THE YETI

Tim Collins

Illustrated by Abby Ryder

D1424345

THE APE
TIM COLLINS & ABBY RYDER

THE DINOSAUR
TIM COLLINS & JAMES LAWRENCE

THE SQUID
TIM COLLINS & JAMES LAWRENCE

THE YETI
TIM COLLINS & ABBY RYDER

THE CRAB
TIM COLLINS & JAMES LAWRENCE

THE CYCLOPS
TIM COLLINS & ABBY RYDER

Badger Publishing Limited, Oldmedow Road,
Hardwick Industrial Estate, King's Lynn PE30 4JJ

Telephone: 01438 791037
www.badgerlearning.co.uk

The Yeti ISBN 978-1-78837-348-7

2 4 6 8 10 9 7 5 3 1

THE YETI

Tim Collins

Illustrated by Abby Ryder

Contents

Badger
L E A R N I N G

Story Vocabulary
pieces
scared
swiped

The story so far...

Jade was stuck on the island.

She was climbing up the rocks.

"Welcome to Monster Island," said a voice from below. "I am the Captain. You will never escape."

Jade was angry. She thought the Captain was trying to trick her.

"Why is it called Monster Island?" she asked.

"You will soon find out," said the Captain.

Chapter 1

Snow

Jade began to climb up some steep rocks.

There might be a boat on the other side of the island, she thought.

Then Jade heard someone laughing.

She looked down and saw the Captain.

"You are making a big mistake," he shouted. "Come back!"

But Jade thought the Captain did not want her to find a boat.

So she went on climbing.

It was getting colder and colder.

Then it began to snow.

Jade saw a cave.

I will wait in that cave until it stops snowing, she thought.

As Jade walked into the cave she heard a snap.

She looked down.

Jade had stepped on a pile of bones.

The bones had snapped into small, sharp pieces.

On top of the bones was a human skull.

Chapter 2
The Cave

Jade was scared.

She had to get out of the cave.

She turned to go but there was a dark shape at the front of the cave.

It was a huge Yeti.

It had white fur, angry red eyes and very sharp claws.

The Yeti walked into the cave.

Jade stood by the wall of the cave.

Maybe the Yeti will not see me, she thought.

The Yeti got closer and closer.

It walked right past Jade.

Its long fur brushed her face.

The Yeti's fur made Jade's nose itch.
She couldn't stop herself.

ATISHOO!

The Yeti turned to look at Jade.

Its red eyes burned and it roared.

Chapter 3

Escape

The Yeti swiped at Jade with its claws.

Jade felt the sharp claws scratch the skin on her neck.

What can I use to fight back? thought Jade.

She looked down and saw the sharp bones.

She grabbed a bone and stabbed it into the Yeti's leg.

The Yeti roared.

It tried to swipe its sharp claws at Jade's face.

Jade bent down and picked up another bone.

She stabbed it hard into the Yeti's arm.

The Yeti roared and fell down to the floor.

Jade rushed out of the cave.

Blood dripped from her neck.

I won't make it, she thought.

The Yeti was getting closer and closer.

But its white fur was also dripping with blood.

Jade looked over the edge of the rocks.

She began to climb down.

The Yeti gave an angry roar.

It was too weak to climb down the rocks.

The Captain was at the bottom of the rocks.

"Ha! Ha! Ha!" he laughed. "I see you met my furry friend. I did try to warn you."

Jade had got away from the Yeti, but she was still stuck on Monster Island.

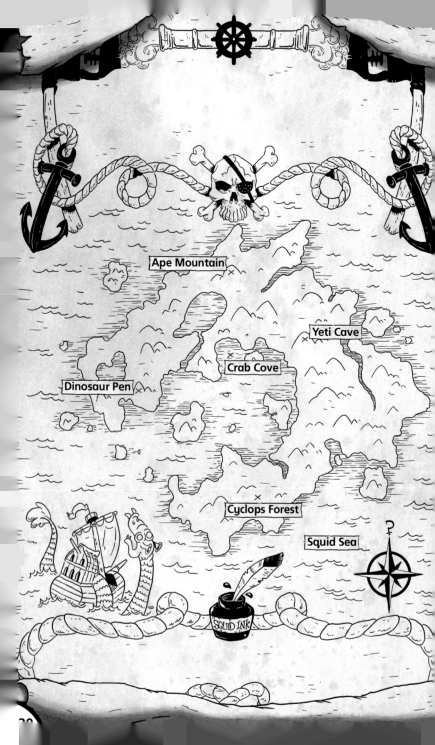

Questions

Chapter 1

What is Jade looking for? *(page 6)*

What does Jade see on top of the pile of bones? *(page 12)*

Chapter 2

Why can't Jade run out of the cave? *(page 13)*

How does the Yeti know Jade is in the cave? *(page 16)*

Chapter 3

How does Jade attack the Yeti? *(page 21)*

Do you think the Captain really wants to help Jade?

About the Author
Tim Collins has written over 70 books for children and adults.

He lives near Oxford and spends his time listening to rock music and playing Pokémon.

He went to a real desert island once, but he didn't see any monsters.

About the Illustrator
Abby Ryder is a cartoonist who loves comic books and video games.

She hopes to one day become best friends with a giant robot.

Hi Lo